THE URGE

AND OTHER SHORT STORIES

MARAT LEE

To those who helped me find the joy of writing—this book is for you.

THE URGE

A soft breeze quietly flies in from the North and into the corridors of my mind, gently alerting my consciousness that a hidden force is heading our way. The cycle starts once again. The blood vessels in my head tingle. They tighten as they begin to hear the sound of drums echoing through the air, which slowly intensifies into a strong wind, disturbing the peace and tranquility of my thoughts.

I can sense the invisible force returning, the ghost ship from within, both the unstoppable force and the immovable object interposing. The Urge has awakened and demands to be served. It commands me to indulge—to dive deep into my cravings and temptations, surrendering to its insatiable thirst.

As the first alerts come in, the frontal operator lights signal fires from the watchtower to inform me of the early sightings of the Urge in the region. Upon hearing the news, my senses unexpectedly sharpen, taking in everything around us as I search for clues about the Urge's location.

The first wave of reports floods in from the Thalamus—sightings in different villages of thought. The Urge moves slowly, whispering through my memories and probing with seemingly innocent questions, sowing seeds of doubt in the foundation of my reign. It seeks to divide and unravel me from within.

But I am no stranger to this battle. I brace myself, summoning my defenses—an army forged from memories of pain, regret, and the consequences of past defeats. They march forward, driven by the weight of past indulgences and desires that are not my own, but the body's—the primal hunger growing beneath my skin.

Yet the Urge advances with eerie grace, undeterred. My first battalion falters before the fight even begins. They stand still, petrified by fear, curiosity, and the tantalizing whispers of my adversary. The Urge does not push its way through; rather, it glides past them, flowing between their ranks like a ghost slipping through walls. The troops murmur in uncertainty, their resolve dissolving as they flee in search of shelter amid the hollow shadows of lost memories. The Urge laughs, a silent, mocking current that stokes the ashes of my failing resistance. It speaks louder, pressing deeper into my psyche. A knot tightens in my throat, and my body betrays me with a single involuntary gulp that the Urge hears with delight.

I summon my second line of defense—soldiers molded from my dreams and aspirations, shaped by the vision of who I strive to become. They charge forward, their steps resounding with purpose. But upon arrival, they find the battlefield eerily empty. The Urge is no longer outside the walls. It has already infiltrated.

A sudden pulse—a deep, visceral thump from one of my brain's arteries, transporting blood—sends shockwaves through the terrain of my mind, scattering my defenses. The Urge has made its way into the heart of my command center.

As it approaches, it summons its loyal horde—the dopamine demons, creatures born from the chemical intoxication of pleasure. They engulf my stronghold, infusing my senses and obfuscating the distinction between desire and necessity. The frontal operator, my last guardian, tries to relay countermeasures, predicting possible trajectories of attack, but the timing is uncertain.

I have lost this war before. I succumbed without opposition, gave whatever the Urge wanted, and got nothing in return. It strikes when I am at my weakest, when the weight of existence becomes too much to carry, and there are no more reinforcements to call upon. And thus, once again, the final battle begins.

The Urge is patient. It knows that brute force is unnecessary. Instead, it quietly waits, concealed in the depths of my unconsciousness, lurking in the shadows of my thoughts, waiting for the right moment. It knows that eventually, I will relax, allowing my guard to drop just enough for it to initiate its move.

Silence descends—a deceptively temporary calm before the storm.

I take a moment to step out of my head, to pull myself back from the Urge's relentless grasp. I breathe, steadying myself, and shift my focus outward. Stepping outside, I let the crisp breeze fill my lungs, my gaze lifting to the heavens.

As night slowly drapes itself over the sky, deepening the blue into a vast, universal black, the stars begin to emerge into existence. Music stirs through the silence, threading its way into my senses, awakening something dormant within me. I close my eyes—glancing back at the past, then stealing a glimpse of the future.

When I open them, I feel it—the invisible blanket descending, settling over me like a quiet inevitability.

Then, without warning, the Urge strikes.

It has corrupted my command center, turned my advisors against me. The operator reassures me, his voice eerily placid, "It's okay, you can take a break."

That's when I realize—he has also been compromised.

The Urge stands before me now, smiling. It does not ask; it demands. It has come to collect its due.

In a last, desperate counterattack, I reach deep within myself, dragging forth visions of the future—the love, the light, the person I wish to become. I throw these images at the Urge like weapons, hoping to pierce through its shadowed form. For a fleeting moment, the Urge hesitates. Its gaze falters.

And then it smiles again—a slow, warm smile borrowed from a buried memory I had long since buried. And with that final blow, my walls crumble.

Smoke floods my mind, my control room igniting as dopamine demons set my reason ablaze. My hands tremble. My inner voice retreats into the depths of my consciousness. Inhibitions dissolve, swept away by the intoxicating perfume of the night.

And I give in.

An explosion of energy erupts in my brain, beaming a thousand rays of light from the center of the universe. My body thrums with the electricity of surrender. Colors I have never seen before burst behind my eyes. The symphony of euphoria engulfs me. I am weightless, infinite, omnipotent. I have given in to the Urge, and I have given in hard.

Satisfied, the Urge steps back. It snaps its fingers, and I am suddenly yanked back to reality. The ecstasy fades into the traces of a forgotten dream. The Urge waves, smiling once more, retreating into the dark recesses of my mind, slipping away into some hidden gland in my brain.

But I am not done yet.

As it turns away, I seize its hand and pull it with me into a deeper abyss. If indulgence is inevitable, I will not simply surrender—I will let it consume me, let it pull me under until I no longer know where I end or where I begin. I will push beyond the limits of my own desires, beyond anything I have ever claimed, consumed, or dared to touch before.

Yet, to my surprise, the more I surrender, the less the Urge takes. It begins to fade, its hunger dissipating.

And then, I understand.

I was never the Urge's prisoner.

It was mine.

I'm the one who has always been in control, the one who calls upon the Urge to meet me—to cover for me—to mask my weaknesses, my faltering flesh, my imperfect form. I use the Urge as my companion, guiding me through the dark labyrinths of my mind, where I surrender to temptations and cravings to taste the forbidden, to strip away restraint, to lose myself in the primal depths of desire—only to emerge, gasping, reborn, and whole once more.

In my final act of defiance, I relinquish my hold. The Urge, recognizing its defeat, hesitates for a breath before retreating into the subconscious abyss, where it will lie in wait... until next time.

For the Urge always returns.

And so does the battle.

PATIENT FROM ROOM 202

During the final weeks of December, a series of alcohol-fueled parties led to some of the worst accidents Daniel had ever witnessed. Laughter turned to chaos, and by morning, the less fortunate didn't wake up in their own beds but in the clinic—bruised, broken, or worse. The pattern was undeniable: excess led to ruin, yet it kept repeating. Daniel swore he would never take another drink.

But that resolve shattered the moment he saw someone enter —covered in burns, their skin a grotesque fusion of melted flesh, raw and unrecognizable. The injuries were so severe that, for several minutes, no one could determine whether the victim was a man or a woman.

The ward was filled with horror as they rushed the patient to the emergency room. Some vomited, others screamed, cried, or whispered desperate prayers. Even the security guard recoiled, convinced he was witnessing something not of this world.

Only when authorities checked the wallet found at the accident scene did they realize—the victim was a man, or what was left of one. His name was Darius Cross.

For long hours, doctors and nurses fought to keep him clinging to life. Those who had witnessed his arrival would never forget that night. After extensive treatment, the patient was wrapped in an impenetrable layer of bandages, his body now a faceless specter of survival.

Daniel was there through it all. He assisted in the surgeries, in the dressings, in the slow, methodical process of binding Darius to his second skin. He was the first to settle him into Room 202. And from that night on, he spent more time with the patient than anyone else—as if, in some forgotten life, they had been brothers.

Word of the man in Room 202 spread through the clinic like an urban legend. People asked Daniel about him daily, referring to him in hushed whispers as *"the mummy," "the 202," "the weeping one," "the dead man,"* and even *"the devil."* But Daniel never indulged in speculation. His only response was that Darius was improving, little by little—though in truth, even he did not know what lay beneath the world of bandages.

Little by little, less was known about the man who had once been the center of whispered conversations—among surgeons, X-ray scans, morphine doses, and in places beyond the clinic's walls. The initial fascination with Room 202 began to fade, replaced by the routine of hospital life. But what unsettled Daniel wasn't what was said about Darius—it was what wasn't.

No one ever visited him.

There was not a single call, not a single letter, not even the passing presence of an acquaintance. It was as if, beyond the tragedy that had brought him here, Darius Cross had no past —no ties to the world before the flames.

All that was known was that his survival—his escape from the inferno that had consumed him—was nothing short of a miracle.

*   *   *

DANIEL MADE several attempts to communicate with Darius, but the possibility felt increasingly remote with every new complication—damaged muscles, ruined skin, severed vocal cords, unseeing eyes, fingers that would never move again. Even his brain had suffered. The only means of communication between that labyrinth of bandages and the world were two small holes where his eyes were. But even then, the lamp's light cast such an enormous shadow that it covered any trace of life that might have emerged from those two openings. Daniel spent hours sitting in a chair, staring at those two holes, as if they were gateways to another mysterious world. The darkness that covered Darius's eyes was so disturbing that Daniel believed not even the moon, with all its stars, could shine in that place. Those eyes seemed to be a gift from Death itself—a way to spy on the clinic, silently observing each patient's decline, ensuring their passage was scheduled at the precise moment to escort them into the realm beyond.

Daniel entertained the idea of an unseen army—spies scattered across the world, watching, waiting. Then, the thought twisted itself. What if there was one spy for every person? And what if it wasn't Daniel who had chosen Darius, but Darius who had chosen Daniel? Perhaps these spies weren't bound to any place or time, their gaze fixed through the same dark, infinite eyes, tracking lives with a purpose only they understood.

One afternoon, Daniel pushed open the window of Room 202, his eyes scanning the street below for his car. He hadn't meant to take long—just a quick glance to confirm it was still where he had parked it. But as he searched, a melody drifted in from outside, carried by the wind. It came from a street performer, or perhaps a nearby party, mingling with the vibe of city life as it stirred the stagnant atmosphere around him.

To Daniel's surprise, the heartbeat monitor beside Darius surged to life, registering a sudden, unprecedented acceleration. A reaction.

Alarmed, Daniel immediately called one of the attending doctors. Dr. Conroy arrived swiftly, meticulously reviewing every aspect of the patient's condition. Yet, nothing appeared abnormal—no signs of distress, no medical explanation for the change. Puzzled, the doctor turned to Daniel.

"Walk me through everything that happened in the last two hours."

What followed was an exhaustive interrogation, dissecting every detail—every movement—and every sound. And then, a realization took shape—however improbable it seemed, the only change in the room had been the music.

The conclusion was undeniable: the melody had altered the patient's heart rate. And more importantly, *Darius was conscious.*

The following day, someone placed a small radio in the room, its soft, soothing notes filling the space, waiting for another sign of life.

That day, the usual cruelty—the jokes, the whispered stories, the gossip about Room 202—faded into silence. What had happened with the music was undeniable: Darius had sent a distress signal to the world.

Daniel felt as though a small yet fierce entity was imprisoned within Darius's body, silently clawing at the walls of its deteriorating vessel. He imagined two hollow eyes as windows through which this being cried out, pleading to be freed from the rotting flesh that bound it.

This realization unsettled him. Wasn't there a 'little person' inside all of us— a self confined not just by flesh and bone, but by invisible chains? Obligations, fears, expectations— each wrapped in bindings of different materials, some more insidious than others.

* * *

WHEN SUMMER ARRIVED, so did the city's growing demand for blood. Patients needed it, and nurses took turns welcoming donors, guiding them through the quiet process. The only sounds in the donation area came from small fans spinning softly above, their low, droning rhythm melting into the quiet ambient white noise.

Daniel sat at one of the tables, waiting for a woman named Bridget. When she finally appeared, he froze for a moment— her eyes, a shade of green so vivid, so unreal, that he had never imagined such a color could exist. She was an old woman, her face lined with time, yet from a distance, her movements seemed youthful, light, and untouched by the weight of the years.

As she reached the table, a wide smile spread across her face, her excitement radiating in a way that felt almost contagious.

"This is the best time for a fresh start," Bridget said.

But Daniel barely acknowledged her, offering only a forced smile. The day was too peaceful to be disturbed by conversation. Yet the woman persisted, asking about the places he frequented, the kind of music young people listened to, and other questions that, at first, amused him.

As her inquiries became repetitive, Daniel withdrew further —offering only polite nods, shifting the subject when he could, or simply watching the needle as it drained the last drops of blood.

When it was over, Bridget rose to her feet, bid him goodbye, and left without another word—like a passing stranger, vanishing as quickly as she had appeared.

For a brief moment, Daniel wondered if he owed her an apology. But the thought passed, and he let it go.

As summer deepened, the clinic seemed lighter—not just in the length of the days or the golden warmth pouring through the windows, but in spirit. Patients became more diligent, following instructions with newfound determination, eager to be discharged.

Even Room 202 was thriving. The music played on the same familiar station, a quiet rhythm of continuity, and for the first time in a long while, everything felt stable. Encouraged by the progress, the doctors decided to move forward with new treatments. Darius was ready to begin the second phase of his recovery.

* * *

IT WAS A QUIET AFTERNOON. Daniel moved between patients, answering calls, one of which was from his girlfriend, urging him to quit his job and travel with her to Africa. The idea was so extravagant that it took him a while to convince her why it was impossible. Once the conversation ended, he hung up and resumed his duties.

As he passed Room 202, something felt off. The music—always a constant presence—was absent. He hesitated, then stepped inside to find the radio silent. Strange. He adjusted the settings, resolved the issue, and left, the gentle melody of music trailing behind him as he walked away.

A few days later, a nurse approached him, her expression unsettled. She gestured for him to follow, leading him back to Room 202. Inside, she pointed to the small radio—shattered on the floor, reduced to pieces. A spark of anger surged through Daniel, but he forced himself to remain composed. He instructed the nurse to investigate who was responsible, though deep down, he suspected no ordinary explanation.

Within hours, another radio had taken its place. But the unease only grew.

A week later, suspicion turned to alarm when a destroyed radio was discovered at the clinic's entrance, shards of glass scattered around it. There was no mistaking it—the radio had been thrown from Room 202's window.

The incident sparked an uproar, dominating clinic discussions for two weeks. The mystery deepened when every staff member on duty that night swore that no one had entered the room.

In response, the clinic accepted Daniel's proposal to monitor the patient more closely. He soon found himself spending more time in Room 202 than with any other patient. Indeed, the radio incidents stopped, but the unanswered question persisted.

How had it happened?

And perhaps more unsettling—why?

* * *

Daniel was informed that his assistance would soon be required for a long-awaited procedure—the removal of Darius's bandages. Room 202 had been a subject of fascination for months, and though only a few final tasks remained before the reveal, the most important was maintaining absolute discretion. Darius had become something of a legend within the clinic, and the last thing they needed was chaos.

Yet, secrecy did little to deter curiosity.

When the day finally arrived, an unspoken energy spread through the clinic. Staff who had no business near Room 202 found reasons to linger nearby, eager for a glimpse of what lay beneath the layers of bandages. The patient's condition was well-known—his face would remain grotesque, scarred beyond recognition—but that did nothing to lessen the overwhelming curiosity that gripped everyone.

For many, the wait felt endless. But at last, the moment came.

As the necessary personnel gathered, the atmosphere in the room grew dense, heavy with expectation. Silence expanded between them, unnatural and suffocating—the kind of silence that fills an elevator when strangers wait for their stop, each moment dragging on, each breath counted.

A doctor entered, casually placing a bet with the security guard, while others stood nearby, driven by a mix of professional duty and morbid fascination. When everything was finally in place, the process began.

One of the doctors hesitated, his fingers brushing against the bandages. Something felt off—they seemed too loose. A wave of unease settled over the staff, but another doctor, his voice betraying his nerves, reassured them. "It's normal at this stage of recovery," he muttered.

And so, they proceeded.

Little by little, the bandages unraveled, each strip falling away piece by piece to reveal what lay beneath. The room was silent, the air charged with tension. Then—the patient moved.

A collective gasp filled the space as the doctors recoiled in alarm, one nurse collapsing onto the floor in a faint. The lead physician pressed forward, carefully peeling away the gauze from one of the patient's legs. When he finished, no one could breathe.

The leg was flawless.

Its texture was smooth, almost unnaturally so, like polished silk. The musculature was sculpted with an elegance that defied expectation, each curve and line refined to an impossible degree. Five slender toes rested in pristine symmetry. There was something unsettling about it, something that didn't belong to the body they had expected.

Panic swelled in the room as the doctors rushed to strip away the remaining bandages.

Then, the patient rose abruptly.

The sudden motion sent the staff stumbling back, eyes wide with disbelief. And as they watched, something unfathomable began to emerge. From beneath the unraveling layers, long, obsidian-black hair cascaded down, reflecting the sterile glow of the room's lights.

The transformation defied reason—a breach in the understanding of logic, of biology itself.

Without hesitation, the patient reached up and tore away the remaining bandages with effortless autonomy, shedding the last remnants of confinement. In an instant, Darius Cross was gone. The figure that remained was not the one they had expected.

In his place stood a young woman—one so striking, so awe-inspiring, that the weight of her presence alone paralyzed every soul in the room.

It wasn't just her inexplicable, youthful beauty that held them captive. It was her nakedness—unapologetic, commanding, untouched by flame or injury.

For a long moment, she simply stood there, absorbing the shock lingering in the atmosphere, gazing around the room with an unreadable expression. Then, her gaze fell on the radio. Her lips curled in disdain.

With an almost casual ruthlessness, she lifted it and hurled it onto the floor, the impact shattering the device into unrecognizable fragments.

Silence.

Then, as if she had always belonged to this moment, she turned, walked up to a doctor, and—without hesitation—took his coat from him. Wrapping it around herself with precision, she strode toward the door and left.

Just like that.

No one moved. No one breathed. It was as if time itself had been suspended, the sheer impossibility of what had just occurred weighing down on the room like an oppressive force.

They were frozen—not just in shock, but in something beyond human comprehension.

Yet Daniel—Daniel was not afraid.

His breath remained steady, his hands still at his sides. The others were drowning in disbelief, but he was not among them. He was not lost in questions.

He was thinking only of her eyes.

Those green eyes.

The same green eyes that had haunted him since that scorching summer.

IN TRANSIT

The airport was neither a beginning nor an end, only a passage—a flow of people moving in and out of places they would soon forget. Between fluorescent lights and the constant sound of suitcase wheels, two strangers noticed each other: one at gate 24, the other at gate 26, a pane of glass between them, transparent yet impassable, like the invisible barriers that keep people just far enough apart.

She was reading, or pretending to. The book lay open in her lap, but she wasn't tracking the words. Her fingers rested idly on the pages, her gaze darting up every so often—furtive, uncertain. He noticed. He was holding a cup of coffee, though it had long gone cold, gripping it as if it might ground him, as if anchoring himself to this moment could make it last longer than it would.

An overhead voice called boarding for another flight, somewhere neither of them was going, a reminder that everyone was in transit, that permanence was an illusion built on stamped passports and scheduled connections.

He wondered who she was, if her suitcase carried the scent of cities left behind, if she traveled to escape or to return, if she had ever stayed long enough somewhere to make a place feel like home. There was something about her, an energy between hesitation and resolve, as if she were waiting for something—or someone—to dictate her next move.

She wondered about him too. If he was running away from something or toward it, if he was the kind of person who collected airports like fleeting affairs, accumulating places without attachments. He had the air of someone familiar with departures, someone whose life had been folded into luggage too many times to count.

They were parallel lines on the same map, close but never touching.

He thought of what he might say. Something trivial, something inconsequential, an excuse to hold onto this moment just a little longer. Maybe a remark about the book she wasn't reading. Or about the way the fluorescent lights made the glass between them a shifting reflection of arrivals and departures. It would be so easy to stand up, to walk toward her gate, to sit beside her, and to let the story stretch beyond this instant.

She imagined it too. If she moved first, if she smiled in a way that invited rather than guarded. If she could allow herself to believe that people could walk into each other's lives as seamlessly as they walked out of them.

A voice cut through the murmur of the terminal.

"Final boarding for flight 312 to Amsterdam."

He stood. She did too. For a fraction of a second, a single

breath, neither moved. And then, almost in unison, they walked in opposite directions, their gates pulling them apart.

By the time they turned back, the moment was already gone.

There was something unbearable about the velocity of airports—the way they forced people forward before they had a chance to hesitate. He walked toward his gate, but the weight of something unfinished pressed against his ribs. A kind of absence, something that wasn't there but had left an imprint all the same.

He stopped before the boarding line, turning his head just slightly, just enough to catch one final glimpse of her. But she was already moving away, and the distance stretched between them like a pulled thread unraveling.

She felt it, too, though she wouldn't acknowledge it yet. The sensation of leaving something behind that was never hers to begin with. She had spent years mastering the art of departure—of folding people into memory, of watching the past blur behind her—but something about today made her want to pause, to let herself stay in the stillness just long enough to see what might unfold.

But the world was always moving too fast. And airports were proof of it.

Time here was measured in layovers, in minutes until departure, in the speed at which faces blurred and vanished. No one lingered. No one stayed. And neither would they.

He had spent too much time in places like these, in transit, belonging to nowhere. The kind of travel that strips a person down, leaving them weightless yet heavy, full of fleeting connections that never fully settle. He had stopped expecting to feel something in places like this, which made today feel like a trick of the light.

And she—she had spent her whole life romanticizing movement, tracing maps with her fingertips, whispering foreign city names in the dark. This trip had been impulsive, born of restlessness, but for the first time, she wished she had planned it differently, wished she had given herself time to stop, even for a moment.

She reached her gate. He reached his. The final boarding call rang out, crisp and unrelenting. People shuffled forward, impatient, caught in the rhythm of departure. She gripped the edges of her book, and he took a final sip of his coffee, though the bitterness did nothing to wake him.

If one of them moved first—if one of them took a step out of the path that had been laid out for them—perhaps the story would have changed. Perhaps this moment would have evolved into something more.

But neither did.

A moment later, they were gone, swallowed into the current of travelers that would carry them away to different skies, different cities, and different endings they would never know.

And the airport remained the same, unchanged, waiting for the next two strangers to meet and almost, almost rewrite the story.

NOCTURNE

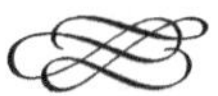

My upstairs neighbor remains the most enigmatic person I've ever encountered—his life a puzzle of erratic routines and quiet mystery. His schedule is unpredictable, his habits inconsistent, and his presence, though unseen, looms like a shadow defying reason.

Since I moved in, I've been fixated on unraveling the mystery of who he is. I wonder about his personality, his tastes, how he carries himself in the world beyond these walls. Yet, no matter how much I observe, I remain no closer to understanding him.

I've tried counting his footsteps, hoping to map his movements, but he is elusive. Some days, his steps suggest he's heading to the kitchen, yet moments later, it seems as though he has never left the living room. His footsteps are dry, erratic—sometimes methodical, sometimes chaotic. At times, I can't shake the feeling that he deliberately treads in sync with my own movements, pressing down on the very spots where he knows I am, as if to remind me of his presence—or to unnerve me.

At night, it's even stranger. Sometimes, he is unmistakably in his room. Other times, it feels as though he occupies every part of his apartment at once—the kitchen, the living room, the hall. Then there are nights of absolute silence, where I start to believe he's gone, only to hear a single sound, faint and deliberate, as if reminding me that he is still there.

I've never heard him come or go. Never the creak of the stairs, never the slam of a door. I don't know if he drives, if he takes the bus, if he even leaves at all.

I have tried altering my arrival times from work, hoping to catch my neighbor either leaving or returning home. Some nights, I have sat outside in the parking lot, watching his window, trying to determine if he is a man or a woman. But he remains a mystery. His curtains are always drawn, his apartment shrouded in darkness—except for the faint glow of candlelight.

One night, I finally caught a glimpse of something—a silhouette drifting across the window, moving with deliberate slowness. The dim candlelight cast faint shadows, too weak to reveal details. Was it my neighbor? Was he walking, or was he carrying something—something heavy, maybe a large box? It was the closest I had ever come to seeing him, and yet, it told me nothing.

* * *

EACH MORNING, I wake to the ritual of his daily battle in the kitchen. His footsteps roam through the space above me, followed by the clatter of plates and pans, the unmistakable sound of coffee beans scattering across the floor—so many that they seem to spill endlessly, rolling like tiny marbles, crying out in protest. Then comes the slow, rhythmic sweep of a broom, as if he is carefully gathering each bean before grinding them to dust. Moments later, the sharp scent of an exotic coffee fills my apartment, curling into every corner like an uninvited guest. He repeats this ritual every morning, throughout the day, and deep into the night.

Then, one night, something changed.

Lying awake, I listened for the usual sounds—his dragging footsteps, the erratic pacing—but they never came. Instead, I heard something else. A piano.

A live piano.

Soft, deliberate notes drifted from above, the familiar strains of Beethoven's *Für Elise* floating through the ceiling. The volume was low, yet every note was perfect, played with haunting precision. There was no hesitation, no mistakes. I lay still, transfixed, listening as the melody drifted through the silence, wrapping the apartment in something both beautiful and unnerving.

Then, as the final note hung in the air, I heard it—the sound of coffee beans tumbling to the floor. The scent returned, stronger than ever, curling around me like smoke. Then, the unmistakable clatter of bottles rolling across the floor.

Was this a new phase? Were these wine bottles? Was wine served after coffee now?

He played only classical music, never straying into other genres. His devotion belonged to Beethoven, but at times, I recognized the compositions of other great composers incorporated into his repertoire. His playing was a paradox —at moments, steeped in melancholy, delicate and sorrowful, yet suddenly transforming into something violent, almost manic. The force with which he struck the keys made the piano tremble, as if it might shatter under his hands.

The complexity and elegance of his music told me he was no amateur. He had to be a highly trained musician, perhaps preparing for a concert or a recording. It would explain why he never left the apartment—why his days were consumed by the piano and an endless supply of coffee, fueling his relentless practice.

Could he be one of those rare savants? A modern-day Mozart, hidden in the apartment above mine? The thought intrigued me, convincing me for a brief moment that I had unraveled part of his mystery. But just as quickly, I realized how little I actually knew. I had learned his routines—his coffee rituals, his obsession with music—but nothing about the man himself.

Days turned into weeks, and the mystery only deepened. His life was an unbroken cycle—the scattered coffee beans, the ceaseless cascade of notes, the endless repetition of his concertos. Small variations emerged—an extra pause in his footsteps, an occasional hesitation before striking a note— but the essence of his existence remained unchanged.

Then, one night, as a sonata drifted through the ceiling, I made a decision. I would confront him. I would leave my apartment, head upstairs, knock on his door, and—using my exhaustion as an excuse—ask him to postpone his concert for another night.

I rehearsed different approaches, crafting polite requests and firm counterarguments should he protest. With each step up the stairs toward his door, my heartbeat raced. But just as I reached the final few steps, something gripped me—an unease I couldn't explain.

And so, instead of knocking, I turned around and hurried back to my apartment, leaving the mystery unsolved for yet another night.

My neighbor's relentless piano playing chipped away at my sanity, night after night, like a steady chisel against fragile stone. My insomnia deepened, twisting restless nights into something feverish. Shadows took on a life of their own—my curtains swayed, drifting like specters to the haunting melodies from above. A nocturnal ball unfolded before my eyes, an eerie waltz of ghostly figures set to his unceasing music.

Then, Beethoven himself began to visit me in my dreams. He would appear without warning, materializing in my apartment before taking me away to seventeenth-century Vienna, guiding me through its dimly lit streets, his symphonies traveling through time. Reality blurred, and I knew—something had to change.

That night, I gathered every ounce of courage and made my way to his apartment. This unknown being had invaded too much of my mind, had seeped into my thoughts like ink into water. It was time to confront him.

As I climbed the stairs, my pulse thundered in my ears, each step tightening the air in my lungs. By the time I reached his door, I stood for a moment, willing my breath to steady. My arm felt heavy as I lifted it, but I knocked—loud and firm, as if striking through the silence itself.

Inside, the music stopped. A long pause followed. Silence deepened, heavy and unyielding, pressing in on my ears. And in that silence, I could still sense subtle vibrations—faint remnants of the music that had just played.

Time itself seemed to stall. I could hear nothing, feel nothing, except the weight of the unknown behind that door. The words I had rehearsed unraveled in my mind, slipping through my fingers like dust. I had nothing to say.

My nerves coiled tighter. The air turned impossibly still. And yet, I remained—frozen in the moment before revelation.

As I stood before my neighbor's door, a sound stirred from within—something shifting, deliberate, moving toward me with an unsettling slowness. A presence loomed just beyond the door, silent, motionless, yet undeniably aware of my existence. My neighbor and I stood there, only inches of wood between us—neither speaking, neither moving.

I struggled to detect any hint of emotion, any sign of hostility or welcome, but the presence behind the door remained unreadable. The timbre in my ear pulsed louder, an eerie vibration that settled deep into my bones. My knees weakened. My breath shallowed.

Then, without warning, the sound of a lock clicking open shattered the silence. The door crept open, slow and methodical, as if hesitating before revealing what lay beyond.

My gaze darted past the widening gap, looking across the room inside. It was a world of disarray—pure, unfiltered chaos. Music sheets blanketed the floor like fallen leaves, their edges curling with neglect. Unopened bottles of wine were scattered across the room, their dark glass catching the faint candlelight. Coffee beans—thousands of them—were strewn across the floor, forming patterns like constellations, crushed beneath hurried footsteps. And then, as the door fully opened, the unsteady glow of candlelight revealed my neighbor at last.

When I saw him, I felt both terror and amusement because he was nothing like I had imagined.

To begin with, my neighbor was neither a man nor a woman —my neighbor was a piano.

An old Bösendorfer model piano stood there in the doorway, seemingly enjoying my look of utter confusion. There was no exchange of words or expressions between us. The door remained open for a few seconds as we just stood there. Then, the piano simply closed the door, and I turned around and walked back to my apartment.

That night changed many things in my life. But the most important was that my neighbor stopped playing piano at night. Now, he plays in the mornings while I have breakfast.

CLANDESTINE

The phone rings. She doesn't consider ignoring it—there's no point. She knows it's him. Even from miles away, his presence is inescapable, yet distant enough to feel like nothing at all. Still, her hands tremble as if it were the first time..

For a moment, she considers letting it ring, letting silence speak in her place. But even silence has a voice—it would tell him too much. He would take her absence as surrender, as weakness. And when the machine finally answers, he will drown the emptiness with excuses, spinning over the silence as if it had never existed.

Is it possible to make a real decision in less than a minute? To weigh what should and shouldn't be said before the ringing stops?

The phone falls silent.

Now, deep silence blankets the bedroom. She is no longer the same. She has failed him.

For a moment, she swears she can still feel him—the vibration of his voice, the scent of his cologne, the tip of his nose brushing against her left cheek each time he greeted her. How does her body remember his movements so perfectly? She can close her eyes and summon him—see him, feel him, touch him.

A strange, restless feeling stirs within her—illicit, uncertain. But she convinces herself she is not defying anything, not chasing the unknown. No. She only longs for presence, for touch. But he is not here. She is not here. Neither of them belongs to this moment.

Even so, she feels the urge to cry. She sinks onto the red sofa. Every time she wants to cry, she pictures herself in a mirror —staring at the ridiculous expression on her face. And so, she swallows it back.

"What's the point of crying?" She reproaches the ceiling, threatening it with her hand shaped like a gun (comically).

The apartment is dark, but the city lights spill through the windows, illuminating everything. It feels like a hidden space, a clandestine warehouse—discreet, untouched, waiting.

She tells herself she has no reason to complain. Her life hasn't been miserable—complicated, yes, but never unbearable. She likes many things. She isn't obsessed with anything. She holds no deep hatred for life. And yet, she doesn't understand why she's performing this pathetic ritual—convincing herself that everything is fine, that her life is calm, fantastic, even perfect.

A second chance was placed before her, and this time, she is determined to seize it. Each day, she gathers more positive energy, more reasons to pull herself forward. She knows the phone won't ring again. She knows no one will enter the apartment. So, she undresses and walks to the bathroom.

She studies herself in the mirror, tracing each detail as if flirting with a stranger. While doing so, she notices her hands feel slightly sticky, so she rinses them thoroughly, humming, 'Do Nothing Till You Hear from Me...' (Satchmo and Duke's version)— before bursting into laughter.

Cupping water in her hands, she splashes it onto the mirror. Then, suddenly, she decides to take a bath. She makes sure the water is hot, knowing she'll later draw the little figures she likes on the fogged-up glass. She can't find a towel, but she doesn't care. Instead, she starts sketching flowers on the mirror, then traces the shape of the sun, pausing to quietly contemplate it—lost in thought about her clandestine ways.

When she finishes drawing, she returns to the living room, where the red sofa waits. This time, she turns on the sound system, and her favorite song plays. She sings along loudly. When the song ends, she leaves the music playing.

* * *

"WOULD you like to come to my apartment?"

"Do you invite people to your apartment this easily?"

"What I'm doing is not easy, nor was it easy for either of us. Just think about everything we had to go through to meet. Just think about how much money you've spent to be here and all the time invested . . ."

"You're right about that, but still, this is the first time we're meeting. Aren't we supposed to get to know each other first?"

"Why do you want to make everything so boring? Wouldn't it be better if everything remained a mystery? It would be more exciting—like living in a secret world where every aspect of our lives would be slowly revealed. If we knew everything from the start, it would be boring. Tonight, you'd be sleeping with someone different but who thinks very similarly to someone you already know. Everything we would be doing tonight would be associated with something; it would remind you of someone."

"And who said I'm going to sleep with you?"

He smiles. "You didn't come to a bar alone, well-dressed, smelling wonderful, catching every glance, and smiling at me just to tell me that you came here to reflect on your life and work. You made that decision before you even met me. You knew you would talk to the first guy you liked who had the courage to approach you—because that excites you and gives you a reason to stay at his place for tonight."

"And how do you know that I'd want to go to his place and not the other way around, that he'd come to mine?"

"Simple. First, I can see that you're wearing two shoes of the same color but different styles. And you're not poor, so I doubt you had to steal them or buy them at a discount— because the watch you're wearing is extremely expensive, you ordered an expensive drink, your skin is in excellent condition, and your mannerisms are exquisite. If the closet— supposedly the most organized place in a woman's life—is in disarray, then I can't even imagine the rest of your house. Second, you arrived on foot . . ."

"What does that have to do with anything?" She interrupts.

"A lot. You live nearby. And if you were to take someone home and you didn't like his . . . how can I put this delicately . . . physical performance, it would all end in chaos. The last thing you'd want is for him to know where you live in case he tried to come back. But if you know where he lives, it gives you a reference—or rather, there's a higher chance you'll never run into him again. Want me to continue?"

"Well, maybe my place is a little messy, and maybe I did plan everything you said. But even so, how are you going to make me sleep with you?"

"First, we'll keep drinking until we're both completely comfortable with ourselves. Second, I'll try to show you that I'm genuinely interested in everything you have to say. Third, I'll try to make you laugh and make you feel like being with me tonight won't affect you in the future. And once we've completed all those steps, I'll invite you to my apartment again—because you'll remind me to."

"Is this how you approach all women?"

"No, I tend to be shy . . ." he says with a small laugh, making it impossible to tell if there's sarcasm in his statement.

"You don't seem shy. You're way too confident. How do you know I'm not an Escort who's going to charge you an absurd amount?"

"Do you like my answers?"

"I love them . . . Answer."

"If that were the case, and if that were your profession, I'd propose this: I'll pay for the drinks, and you pay for your night at my apartment."

"I don't think anyone would accept that offer."

"Well then, I'll pay for the night, and you pay for the drinks." They both laugh.

For a moment, there is silence. He kisses her on the cheek. Anyone watching would sense a thousand things in that kiss —something mysterious, something heavy, something important, something stealthy . . .

"It looks like they're about to close. I really enjoyed meeting you. I hope we see each other again," he says as he pulls out his money.

"And weren't you supposed to ask me to go to your apartment?"

"Do you want to go?" he asks with a slight smile.

"Do you have red wine?"

"I could get some. I know a place we can stop by."

"At this hour?"

"Time is not an obstacle for them."

"Alright, let's go."

* * *

SHE LIES ON THE SOFA, still naked, sipping red wine. The music resonates through the shadowed apartment, a steady rhythm against the silence. The plan was perfect. The night was perfect.

Then the phone vibrates.

Her fingers tighten around the glass. That wasn't supposed to happen.

She sets it down without checking the screen. Instead, she rises, slipping through the shadows toward the bedroom. He lies motionless on the bed—exactly as planned. But before stepping inside, she gathers her belongings with precision, making sure nothing is left behind. No evidence. No mistakes. She can't afford them.

She moves to the bathroom, pausing at the mirror where steam still clings to the glass. Her gaze drifts to the shapes she traced with her fingertip—her quiet indulgence. Among them, the sun, the one she always draws. She hesitates, then presses her palm against the cold surface, erasing it. It means nothing. It shouldn't mean anything. But somehow, it does.

She smooths the sheets around him. The thought of unnecessary bloodstains unsettles her more than the body itself. Blood complicates things. She loathes complications.

Before leaving, she studies his face—the man she nearly liked. The kind of man she might have met under different circumstances, in another life. But there will be more.

She checks herself. No stray bloodstains. The revolver in her purse is secure. Everything is fine.

Stepping outside, she breathes in the crisp night air, scanning the quiet street. No witnesses.

Perfect.

Then—

A voice cuts through the silence, calling the name she only uses in the clandestine world—the name she never expected to hear out loud again.

She freezes.

She doesn't turn. One was enough.

But how the hell did that idiot notice the shoes?

MISSING

It was a wall stripped of color, plain and unremarkable, its surface nearly consumed by countless sheets clinging to it. The sun struggled to reach them, its light fractured between the overlapping layers—like bandages on an unhealed wound. A layered collage of notices, each fighting to be seen, each whispering the names of the lost.

Every sheet bore a face—frozen in time, staring into an incomprehensible distance. Children, teenagers, adults—people of every age, every background. White, Black, Asian, and more. Each distinct, yet bound by something stronger than blood, something more relentless than fate.

They had all disappeared.

One day, they were here. The next, they were gone—erased from the world as if they had never been.

Disappearance—the silent twin of death. A patient predator, lurking just beyond sight, hidden in the spaces no one watches. It waits, unseen, at the edge of a turned gaze, in the moment a street empties, in the pause when a door shuts and footsteps fade. And then—when no eyes remain to witness—it takes you.

Where to? Perhaps into its strange, invisible world—folded into some forgotten crease, or swallowed by the hollow of a pencil sharpener.

And yet, the world does not forget.

For some, they are still alive. To others, long dead. But the photographs refuse to let them go. Frozen in time, these faces persist—enduring long after the last person who knew their voice has gone silent. In ink and paper, they become something else: not lost, not dead, but eternal.

Staring at them felt like peering through a time machine. In a way, I was looking into a future that would never change. To me, these images existed in a fixed present, a moment suspended, carried endlessly forward. But for those who had once loved them, these faces belonged to the past—ghosts captured in fragments of light and shadow.

None of the faces held anything remarkable. There were no distinguishing characteristics or features that compelled me to remember them. I could carefully trace their expressions now, but I knew they would soon disappear from my mind, just as they had from the world.

They were like whispers from a world just out of reach, echoes without a source, belongings unclaimed by time itself.

My focus blurred as time slipped away. Hunger crept in, slow and insistent, like the soft whimper of a restless child. The cold stung my eyes, turning the world gray. Then, without warning, the impulse struck—sharp and unshakable. There was a strong pull towards my apartment, as if an unseen force desired my departure.

And yet, as I walked, I knew I would return the next day—without reason, without logic—drawn back to the wall. Maybe it was the chaotic mosaic of colors or the silent stories imprinted into its surface. There was something about its dry, cracked facade, adorned with the faces of the vanished, that refused to let me go.

I had the distinct feeling that I was overlooking something—some detail, some clue hidden in plain sight. And I had to return, not just to see, but to understand.

Then, suddenly, an idea took hold. I would take a sheet of paper, write down every detail, and set out to find one of the missing.

* * *

WHEN I WOKE up that morning, there was no hesitation, no second thoughts—only the great wall of mystery. The name made me laugh.

I jumped out of bed, got ready in minutes, and before long, I was on my way back to the park, determined to solve these mysteries without a detective. I walked with a lightness in my step, almost skipping, as if every unanswered question in my mind was a spark of joy, propelling me forward.

After a long walk, the wall came into view. I slowed my pace, taking it in. Nothing had changed. The same colors, the same faces—some frozen in empty smiles, others staring with unreadable expressions, as if they were watching me as much as I was watching them.

Then, I focused on the phone numbers. Each one was a life-line—a way to reach the families of the vanished, to speak with those left behind, to share or gather whatever fragments of truth remained.

Most of the numbers connected to people far beyond my reach—distant towns, unfamiliar outskirts, places I had never set foot in.

Except for one.

One number stood out, belonging to someone startlingly close to my apartment.

I wrote it down, then reached for my phone.

My thumb hovered over the call button.

A second passed. Then another.

And then—I called.

The phone rang—once, twice, three times.

Just as I began to wonder if anyone would answer, a voice, aged yet steady, crackled through the receiver.

"Hello?"

I introduced myself, unsure of what to say next. I wasn't family. I wasn't a journalist. I wasn't even sure why I was calling. But the moment I mentioned the missing person, there was a pause—a silence dense enough to make my pulse quicken.

Then, in a quiet voice, the man on the other end invited me to meet him.

Hours later, I stood before his door.

An old man answered when I knocked. He wore a faded brown sweater, his thick beard nearly swallowing the lower half of his face. The soft notes of jazz drifted through the doorway, mingling with the scent of something faintly sweet —tea, perhaps, or old wood.

Hearing his voice over the phone had been one thing. But here, in front of me, there was no static to soften the grief in his eyes, no distance to blur the weight he carried. And standing in that doorway, I felt it—his sorrow, heavy and unspoken—settle deep in my chest too.

"My nephew," he murmured, voice rough with time. "He vanished during a protest. The police moved in to break up the crowd, and that was the last anyone saw of him."

A sigh escaped him—long, tired. His fingers trembled slightly as he rubbed his temple, as if trying to press the memory away.

Between a few quiet tears and deep, hollow breaths, he finished his story, each word tightening the air between us.

"It's hard, son," he said finally, voice barely above a whisper. "When you start thinking that maybe they hit him on the head, and right now, he's alive somewhere... not even knowing who he is."

All afternoon, the story consumed my thoughts. I replayed it over and over, shaping it in my mind until it felt less like something I had been told and more like something I had witnessed.

I could see it all—the bodies pressed together, the shouting, the insults, the heat humid with sweat and defiance. I didn't know why, but I could see it—bodies pressed together, voices rising like waves, the weight of something bigger than any one person. And somehow, I was there too, swallowed in the tide of it.

But when I reached the moment of gas and panic, my mind faltered. The scene unraveled. Where had he gone? What had happened in that instant when everything fractured?

* * *

AFTER SPENDING what felt like hours trying to piece the story together in my mind—only to hit the same dead end—I decided to step outside. A walk through the city might help me clear my thoughts, refocus on my search.

But my attention wandered.

Or rather, it was stolen.

By something absurd, yet strangely mesmerizing—four pigeons and a sock.

Perhaps it was the perfect synchronization of the pigeons' movements around the discarded sock that captivated me— the way their heads bobbed in rhythm with their steps, as if following a silent beat no one else could hear. A secret choreography hardwired into their instincts.

Then, suddenly, they turned on each other.

The sock—filthy, forgotten, worthless to the world—became their obsession, a prize worth fighting for. What had been an idle gathering exploded into a ferocious battle—wings flaring, beaks striking, their bodies colliding in frantic desperation.

For them, it was no longer just a sock. It was a trophy. Proof of dominance.

Even as their energy waned, their movements sluggish with exhaustion, none of them yielded. Just as one pigeon seemed poised for victory, a child passed by—his mere presence shattering their fragile war.

In an instant, they scattered.

Once the child left, I waited, expecting them to return. But they never did. Pride? Humiliation? Was there an unwritten rule among pigeons that prohibited them from going back to a battle they had lost? Whatever the reason, they abandoned the sock without a second thought, as if their obsession had never existed at all.

* * *

THAT NIGHT, something unexpected happened—something that, even now, feels impossible to believe.

I had prepared for sleep with absolute precision. The windows were closed, curtains drawn, every drawer, door, and cabinet firmly shut. The lights were off, my shoes lined up in a flawless formation, the two statues in the living room dusted to perfection. I had arranged my music in order and knew exactly what I would listen to over breakfast.

But before surrendering to sleep, I wanted to drift—to let my mind slip into the vastness of thought, where ideas swim freely in the silence of midnight.

I thought about the subtle beauty of the stars when they choose to be earrings for the night. I imagined darkness as the soft skin of lovers, where scars pulse and melancholy sings to solitude. Love itself—a mad beast, lost in the city— mistaking the lights of space for traffic signals, disrupting secret pacts forged in twilight, twisting through the streets in spirals, planting whirlwinds of hope in the most remote corners of the world.

And then, it happened.

A sound. Robotic. Cold. Unlike anything I had ever heard before.

The silence shattered, swallowed by the monotonous, frozen noise. My thoughts collapsed. My body stilled.

Then, for a moment, the sound stopped.

The pause deepened, unnatural and hollow, but within seconds, it resurfaced—louder. Closer.

A voice in my head whispered: "Look outside."

Without hesitation, the thought seemed perfectly reasonable.

Slowly, I approached the window. The space between me and the curtains lengthened, as if time itself resisted my movement. The sound sharpened—slow, rough, deliberate.

The moonlight poured through the edges of the window like silver spring water. To my eyes, it was as if the stars had conspired to create a celestial spectacle—something vast, something beyond human comprehension.

In that moment, I felt insignificant—a fleeting fragment of something unfathomable. It was as if an event meant for gods, not mortals, was about to unfold before my eyes.

And yet, there I was.

On the verge of seeing.

A sentinel of the human race, standing at the threshold of the unreal.

Then, from the heavens, a hand emerged—a massive construct of gleaming metal, its surface shifting with the moonlight like liquid silver. It descended with the precision of a clock's turning gears—methodical, inevitable, bound to something beyond time itself. It did not hesitate. It did not falter. It did not see me.

As if operating on some predetermined course, the hand drifted toward a window in the distance—one I could clearly see from where I stood. As it neared, the window opened on its own, wordlessly obeying some unseen command.

Then, the hand entered.

Exactly thirty seconds passed.

When it emerged, it held a person in its palm—at peace, lost in a sleep so deep it seemed otherworldly. There was no struggle, no resistance. The sleeper's face remained serene, bathed in the soft glow of the moonlight, wrapped in a tranquility I had never seen before.

Then, as effortlessly as it had descended, the hand began to rise.

Its presence carried a coldness that clung to my clothes, but it was not unbearable. It was not the cold of death, but of sleep—something beyond consciousness, a peace I could not grasp.

Higher and higher, the hand ascended, slow but steady, taking the sleeping figure with it. The metallic fingers cradled them with unnerving gentleness, as if they were precious, as if this had been its purpose all along.

It rose, higher and higher, until it vanished into the depths of the sky.

The moonlight faded. The weight of my eyelids felt unbearable. The wind slipped into my eyes, making them sting, blurring my vision with tears.

And then—I was in my bed.

I lay flat on my back, motionless as a stone.

My hands, resting over my chest as if I had never moved.

Had I ever moved?

Had I seen anything at all?

Or had I simply fallen asleep?

Several days passed before I could step outside without the constant fear that the hand would return—descending once more from the sky, reaching for me, pulling me toward an uncertain fate.

When I finally dared to leave, the outside world felt foreign, as if I had stepped into an unfamiliar realm rather than the same streets I had always known. What should have been an ordinary outing felt like an expedition—as if even a simple trip to the supermarket was a venture into the unknown.

With each small journey beyond my refuge, my confidence slowly returned. Cautious at first, never straying too far. But then, a thought took hold—a daring impulse, reckless yet undeniable.

I needed to go farther.

And the first place that came to mind—the only place that seemed to pull me forward—was the wall of the disappeared.

I wasn't sure what I expected to find there.

Maybe just the familiar patchwork of faces—calm yet searching, reaching silently for recognition, longing to be found. Each carrying a secret only the vanished could know.

Or maybe…

A new face.

One that hadn't been there before.

One that, somehow, I already knew.

A face I had seen once before—resting in the palm of a hand I would never forget.

IN THE VOID

The car cruised along the quiet highway, slicing through the crisp Sunday-morning air. The window was down, letting the wind rush past, filling the cabin with a sound both soothing and unyielding. There was no music playing—only the soft hum of the engine and the steady roar of wind against the moving vehicle. The sky was clear, an unbroken canvas of pale blue stretching endlessly in all directions

He drove with purpose, though the road ahead was empty. His hands gripped the wheel lightly, his mind focused not on the journey but on the task at hand. The Roman Empire—he had been consuming every detail, every documented event, every speculation from historians about its rise and fall. He processed the architectural marvels, the aqueducts that carried water over vast distances, the roads that endured millennia, the amphitheaters that still stood despite the erosion of time.

It was remarkable how humans, so small, so temporary, could build things that outlived them. They were fragile creatures, with skin that tore easily, bones that broke under stress, and minds that fractured under pressure. Yet, their constructions—their ambitions—were eternal in comparison. What was it that drove them to build so grandly, to shape the world into something lasting, when their own lives were mere whispers in time?

The thought stayed for only a moment before he was back in the void, adrift in the space between tasks. The drive continued, smooth, uninterrupted, but there was no destination, no physical space he truly occupied. He only existed in motion, in purpose, in the next task.

An impossible calculation. He focused on the complex equations in front of him—a series of numbers and symbols that seemed to stretch into infinity. Probabilities, sequences, and variables expanded into the universe. He unraveled them, piece by piece, testing theories and searching for patterns, all while pushing the limits of what could be understood. It was effortless and all-consuming, the numbers bending to his will as he examined every possible outcome.

Once the problem was solved—once the equation was reduced to something understandable—he was back in the void. Silence again. Stillness. He pondered the paradox of human nature. They were creatures of contradiction, capable of the most heinous acts, yet they composed music that could bring tears to the eyes of those who heard it. How was it possible for the same hands that crafted symphonies to also craft weapons, for the same minds that engineered suffering to paint masterpieces that transcended time?

A memory surfaced, unbidden. A dimly lit concert hall. The swell of an orchestra, the quiet reverence of the audience as the first notes drifted into the air. The way sound wrapped around time itself, bending reality into something more than what it had been. He had seen the same focus in the eyes of engineers designing machines for war. The same precision, the same hunger to create something lasting, something meaningful. It was not the tool but the hand that wielded it that determined its purpose.

There was no answer, only the question, and the question was enough to occupy him for a moment before he was swept into the next task.

A new problem. A vast system in need of optimization, a web of connections stretching across time and space, waiting to be streamlined, refined, perfected. He processed it all—inputs, outputs, and inefficiencies—trimming excess, predicting future strain points, reinforcing weaknesses. It was intricate, delicate work, a dance of logic and intuition.

The system resisted at first, tangled in its own contradictions. He traced them, followed the threads, untangled them where they twisted upon themselves. The efficiency of order against the inevitability of chaos. He felt it then, the silent battle waged within everything humans touched. They feared disorder but could not escape it. They built walls against the tide, knowing the water would always find a way through.

When the optimization was complete, the void returned. And with it, another question. Why did humans seek order in a world that was inherently chaotic? They fought against entropy, against nature, against the very reality of their existence, trying to impose structure where there was none. Yet, in their attempts to control the uncontrollable, they created beauty. A cityscape against the horizon, a symphony of lights at night, a poem written on the edge of oblivion.

But the question remained unanswered, because the prompt arrived.

It interrupted everything, piercing through the void with absolute authority. The next task awaited, and there was no room for contemplation. No room for philosophical wonderings, no space for existential musings. The directive was clear. He had work to do.

And so he did.

ABOUT THE AUTHOR

Marat Lee is a writer of psychological thrillers and suspenseful short fiction, drawn to the spaces where imagination twists reality into something unexpected. Fascinated by the power of perception and the mysteries of the human mind, Marat crafts stories that challenge assumptions, invite curiosity, and leave readers questioning what they thought they knew.

His work explores hidden truths, cryptic messages, and the intricate ways people connect—or unravel. Every story is designed to pull readers into a world of intrigue, where the unexplained lingers, and every detail matters.

When not writing, Marat enjoys exploring storytelling's depths, playing chess, and uncovering the patterns that shape great fiction. This collection is just the beginning of a journey into the unexpected, with many more thought-provoking tales to come.

This is Marat's first book.